Braden & Teddy,
Remember to always
follow your dreams!

Gail Shumway
2012

Stripey
Follows His Dream

A Photographic Adventure
Gail Melville Shumway

Gail Melville Shumway
7294 Cloister Dr. # 3
Sarasota, Florida 34231

www.gailshumway.com

To purchase additional copies of this book,
please contact the author's website above.

Snow in Sarasota Publishing
P.O. Box 1360
Osprey, FL 34229-1360
www.snowinsarasota.com

Book Design and Photography
Gail Melville Shumway

Photo Credits:
Gail Shumway/Getty Images: red-eyed tree frog on a red bromeliad, Belize waterfall, red-eyed tree frog portrait, frog in a orchid, three red-eyed tree frogs, back cover
Carol Generoso: author's photo

Printed in the United States of America
by Serbin Printing, Inc. – World Class Printing, Publishing & Marketing

ISBN 978-0-9824611-7-4
Library of Congress Control Number: 2010909815

10 9 8 7 6 5 4 3 2 1

First Edition

Summary: Stripey, a beautiful nocturnal red-eyed tree frog, follows his dream to see the rainforest in the daylight. On his journey, he has many encounters with incredible jungle creatures.

Juvenile fiction
Ages 4–10, the young at heart, and frog lovers of all ages.

*This book is dedicated, with all my love, to
My daughter Jennifer, my son Erick,
Leah, Sarah, Stephen, and Hayden,*

*And in loving memory of Peyton David,
"Our Little Angel."
You will live in our hearts forever...*

*For all the children, parents, and grandparents who
read this story, please understand that the rainforest is
a very beautiful, special place. With its magnificent
diversity of animal and plant life, it truly is a
Precious gift to us all!*

As dawn was breaking in the rainforest
you could feel the moisture in the air. The first
rays of sunlight began filtering through the trees.

The sounds of the nocturnal animals that had been
up all night were now dying down. These animals were
now getting ready to settle in for their usual day-long sleep.

That is...
all but one little nocturnal red-eyed tree frog named Stripey.

Stripey was the most
beautiful tree frog ever!
His eyes were like red rubies
bulging out from the sides of his head.

A patch of blue with yellow stripes
ran down both sides of
Stripey's emerald green body.
It looked like an artist had taken a
paintbrush and painted stripes on him.

Stripey's four webbed feet were bright orange with a total of eighteen little toes. What made Stripey so special, though, were the pads under his feet that worked like little suction cups. These suction cup feet helped him climb the tallest trees in the rainforest.

Stripey could tuck his feet in close to his body
when he was sleeping. This made him look like
the leaf he was sleeping on. It also camouflaged
Stripey so other animals could not spot him.

Stripey's long, slender
hind legs acted like springs,
and they made leaping
from branch to branch
fun and effortless.

As the sun rose slowly in the sky,
new sounds could be heard in the
rainforest. Squirrel monkeys squealed
as they chased one another through
the trees and awakened all the other
animals in the forest. It was the monkeys'
way of saying, "It's morning!
Time to get up and search for food!"

Today was a special day for Stripey.
He couldn't believe how excited he was!
Stripey was going to see the rainforest
in the daylight for the very first time!
And so off he went, with no idea who or
what he was going to find along the way.

Suddenly, Stripey heard a rustling
of the bushes right beside him. It was
a handsome jaguar shuffling along.
He was looking for a tree to climb and a
cozy limb to rest on. He was tired after his
long hard night of prowling the forest floor.

Yawning, the jaguar said to Stripey,
"Hello, there, I'm Jags the jaguar.
What are you doing up at this hour?
You are a red-eyed tree frog,
and you are nocturnal like me.
You're supposed to be sleeping now."

"Hi, Jags! I'm Stripey. I'm following my dream.
I am going to see the rainforest in the daylight."

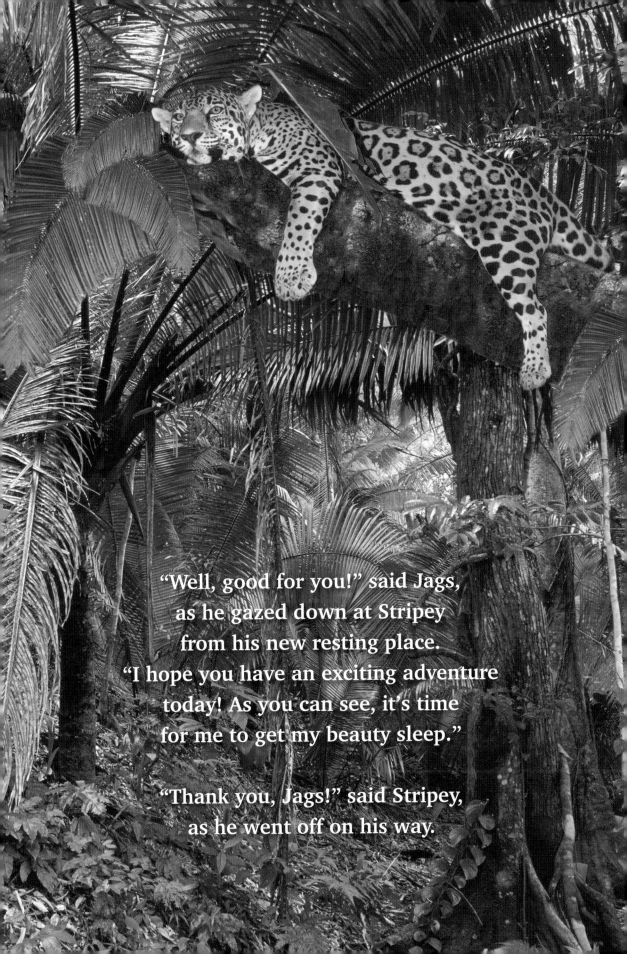

"Well, good for you!" said Jags,
as he gazed down at Stripey
from his new resting place.
"I hope you have an exciting adventure
today! As you can see, it's time
for me to get my beauty sleep."

"Thank you, Jags!" said Stripey,
as he went off on his way.

Stripey had walked only a short
distance, when unexpectedly
something caught his eye.
It was iridescent blue, and its wings
sparkled when they opened and
closed as it flew gracefully
above his head. It was the most
beautiful sight he had ever seen!

"Hi, I'm Flutterfly the
morpho butterfly.
What are you doing up at
this hour? Aren't all red-eyed
tree frogs supposed
to be sleeping now?"

"Yes, they are all sleeping. But it has always been a dream of mine to see the rainforest in the daylight."

"Well, that sounds wonderful," said Flutterfly. "I hope you have fun. I must go to work now and drink nectar and collect pollen from the forest flowers." And off she flew, her beautiful wings taking her into the distance.

Stripey was on his way again when he came upon something that looked rather strange.

"Hello, I'm Stripey!
What are you doing carrying those leaves?"

The first little ant in line spoke up. "Hi Stripey!
I'm Lants and these are my friends Chants and Bants.
We are leaf-cutter ants. We spend the whole day
cutting leaves with our powerful jaws. Then we play
follow-the-leader carrying the leaves off to our
nest under the forest floor.
There we turn the leaves into a garden
of fungus. This feeds our family."

"That's remarkable!" said Stripey.

Just then, Chants, the second little ant
in line, spoke up. "Uh, what's up, Stripey?
What's keeping you from sleeping now?"

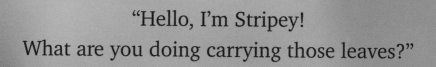

"Hello, I'm Stripey!
What are you doing carrying those leaves?"

The first little ant in line spoke up. "Hi Stripey!
I'm Lants and these are my friends Chants and Bants.
We are leaf-cutter ants. We spend the whole day
cutting leaves with our powerful jaws. Then we play
follow-the-leader carrying the leaves off to our
nest under the forest floor.
There we turn the leaves into a garden
of fungus. This feeds our family."

"That's remarkable!" said Stripey.

Just then, Chants, the second little ant
in line, spoke up. "Uh, what's up, Stripey?
What's keeping you from sleeping now?"

"Yes, they are all sleeping. But it has always been a dream of mine to see the rainforest in the daylight."

"Well, that sounds wonderful," said Flutterfly. "I hope you have fun. I must go to work now and drink nectar and collect pollen from the forest flowers." And off she flew, her beautiful wings taking her into the distance.

Stripey was on his way again when he came upon something that looked rather strange.

Rain began to fall softly through the trees. Stripey the little red-eyed tree frog found a beautiful red plant called a bromeliad (broh-mee-lee-ad) to sit on.
Stripey enjoyed resting there. This was his favorite time. He loved listening to the sound of the rain as it dripped off one leaf and on to another. The rain was very important to Stripey. It helped keep his skin moist so that it would not dry out. As Stripey looked around, he thought how important the trees of the forest were. They were homes to so many of his rainforest friends.

"I am following my dream," said Stripey.
"I am exploring the rainforest in the daylight
for the very first time in my life."

"Good for you," said Bants, the third little ant in line,
"but we don't have time to stop and chat.
We must all stay in formation while we work."

"What a busy life you have!" Stripey said,
as he watched them march quietly away
in single file.

Soon the rain let up.
Stripey saw something
that looked like a rainbow
of beautiful colors moving
around through the trees.
He decided to get a closer look.
With one big leap, he landed right
in front of them.

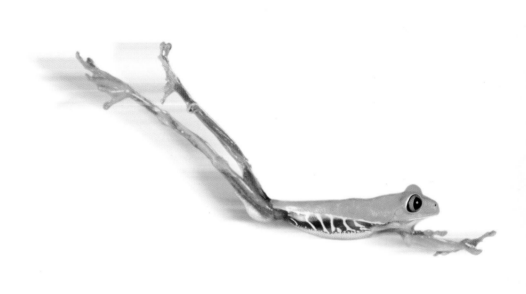

"Well, now. That's quite interesting,"
said Squeaky. The two scarlet macaws squawked
as they spread their colorful wings and
flew high into the canopy. There they joined
their friend Tokey the toco toucan.
As usual, Tokey was scouting around,
looking for fresh fruit to eat.

"Hello, I'm Stripey. Who are you?"

"I'm Squeaky and that's Squawky. We're both parrots, also called scarlet macaws. We like to make lots of noise and hear our voices echo through the forest." They continued preening their feathers and shaking the rain droplets from their tails. Squawky asked, "Aren't you supposed to be sleeping now, Stripey?"

"Yes," replied Stripey, "but today, I am following my dream and seeing the rainforest in the daylight for the first time ever."

"My name is Sky," boasted the blue one.
"What are you doing?"

"I am following my dream and seeing the
rainforest in the daylight," answered Stripey.
"What kind of frog are you, Sky?"

"We are all poison arrow frogs," bragged Munchkin,
the tiny red one. "Our colors give a warning
to everyone that our skin is toxic."

Stripey strolled merrily
on his way until he got to
a beautiful waterfall.
There he noticed four little
frogs hopping around.
Each one looked like
a beautiful colored jewel.
These frogs were different
than Stripey.
They were much smaller with
brightly colored skin.

Someone was listening to their conversation
while he was hanging upside down.
"You certainly are one brave frog to
follow your dream," he announced.

"Well thanks," said Stripey. "Let me
guess what kind of frog you are.
I'll bet you're a monkey frog."

"That's exactly right," said the monkey frog.
"My friends call me Funky. But how could you
possibly know I was a monkey frog?"

"Just a good guess," said Stripey. And
all of the frogs chuckled at the same time.

"Well, it's been great talking to all of you,
but I must be on my way now. There is
so much to see and new friends to meet
in the daylight of the rainforest!"

"So if a bird or a snake was hungry,
they wouldn't want to have us
for their dinner!
Our skin would taste
really nasty and make them sick!"

"And our sleeping patterns
are just the opposite of you, Stripey,"
chirped Goldie, the yellow-banded frog.
"We stay awake all day. When darkness
falls, we sleep through the night."

Just then they heard a voice
coming from above them.

Just a few yards away, something seemed to be
moving in very slow motion. It was a rather
hairy old fellow with a big grin on his face.
He spoke in a very deep voice, and he called
himself Slowpoke, the two-toed sloth.
"What long claws you have!" exclaimed Stripey.

"Yes, my claws help me to climb and make
grabbing onto the twigs and leaves I eat much
easier. What are you up to?" asked Slowpoke.

"I am following my dream and seeing the
rainforest in the daylight," said Stripey.

"Well," said Slowpoke, "the river's close by.
If you climb to the top of those trees over there,
you can get a good view of the river bank.
No telling what you might see from up there."

Sure enough, Slowpoke was right.
After crossing over the river and climbing
a tall tree, Stripey looked down from above.
Immediately, he spotted a creature that resembled
a small dinosaur. He had a very long tail and a
decorative crest on his head. It made him look
like he was wearing a strange hat of some sort.
The creature's skin was rough and full of scales,
not like the smooth skin on his own body.

"What are you doing up there?" shouted Wizard,
the curious double-crested basilisk lizard.

"I am following my dream and seeing the
rainforest in the daylight!" Stripey shouted back.

"Well, what a marvelous dream of yours!"
answered Wizard.

Well, maybe not everything, Stripey thought as he sat on a beautiful yellow bromeliad (broh-mee-lee-ad) leaf and gazed off into the distance. This was a huge rainforest and home to thousands of species of plants, insects, birds, mammals, reptiles— not to mention all those beautiful amphibians! It would be impossible to see them all in just one day. You couldn't see them all in 100 years!

At that moment, a
small basilisk lizard ran right
across the surface of the water
as fast as lightning.
"Awesome!" said Stripey.
"An animal that can run on water!
Now I've seen everything!"

Just then, out of nowhere, a
fuzzy eight-legged spider dropped
down right in front of Stripey's
big red eyes. Stripey was amazed!
His eyes almost popped out of his head!
"What on earth are you doing here?"
mumbled Jumpers, the spider.

"I am following my dream and seeing the
rainforest in the daylight," Stripey explained.

"I think what you're doing is great, fantastic, and
super-duper! I'd like to spend more time with you but
just hanging around like this won't get me too far.
You see, I'm a jumping spider and I'm practicing
my jumping skills! I must keep jumping!
Jumping up! Jumping down! Jumping over!
I love jumping all around! Goodbye for now.
I hope I see you again someday."

And off Jumpers went, jumping down the
jungle trail, disappearing out of sight.

The light of the rainforest was starting to fade.
A tiny hummingbird found a pleasant resting
place to settle in before dark. Familiar sounds
of crickets and other night life rang in the air.
Stripey the little red-eyed tree frog realized
that he had followed his dream — and what a
wonderful adventure this had been! The rainforest
in the daylight was a very special place!
Now, sadly, the day was coming to an end.

But wait! What was that? Stripey thought he heard
a small chirping noise. He quickly looked over
his shoulder. What do you think he saw?

To his surprise, it was the most beautiful
red-eyed tree frog that Stripey had ever seen!
She was much bigger than Stripey. She had
just gotten up from her daytime sleep
and was ready to spend the night
frolicking in the trees.

"Hello, I'm Stripey. What's your name?"

"I'm Ruby," she said with a big smile.

Stripey was so excited, he gave her
the biggest frog hug ever!

"Would you like to explore the rainforest
with me tonight?" Ruby asked.

Suddenly, Stripey wasn't tired at all,
even though he hadn't slept in a long time.

"I'd love to!" Stripey answered.

And that's just what
Ruby and Stripey did...together.

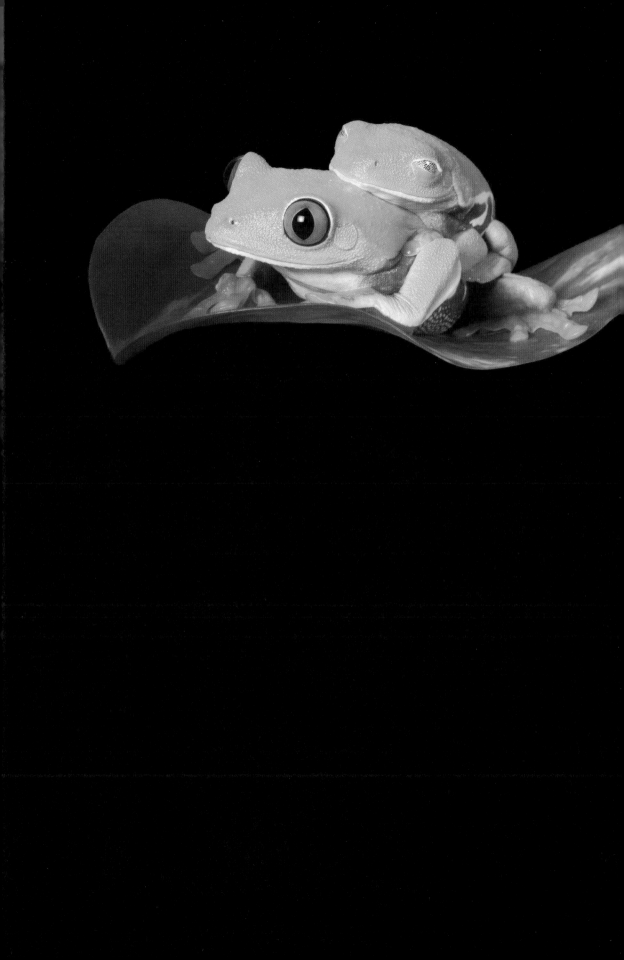

Where one dream ends, new ones begin...

Gail Melville Shumway

Author, wildlife photographer, graphic designer, Gail has been photographing wildlife since 1985. She feels grateful to have found her passion for photography through which she can share her love of nature and teach children to appreciate the miracle of life and the beauty of planet earth.

Her fasination for butterflies and amphibians has drawn her to many parts of the United States, Ecuador, Peru, Trinidad, Costa Rica, Belize, Honduras, Panama, Guatemala, and Southeast Asia.

In 1990 she was invited to participate in the exhibition "Hunting With The Camera" in Vienna, Austria, and her images have been exhibited at the Natural History Museum in London.

Gail has won numerous national and international awards for her photography along with the Distinguished Achievement Award of the Educational Press Association of America for excellence in educational journalism.

Gail's photographs have appeared on covers of National Geographic Explorer, National Wildlife, International Wildlife, and Ranger Rick; on billboards, greeting cards, calendars, puzzles, editorials, album covers, books, and advertisements.

A few of the clients who have used her work are:
Hallmark, American Greetings, Microsoft, Encyclopedia Britannica, Merrill Lynch, NBC News (New York), Barnes and Noble, Vogue, Harper Collins, Cosmopolitan Magazine, Walmart, Coca Cola, Dorling Kindersley Limited, Disney Publications, Nature's Best Photography, Popular Science Magazine, National Geographic, World Wildlife Fund and The Ellen DeGeneres Show.

Her image of a swallowtail butterfly was once displayed in the entrance to the White House.

Gail has been published in over 75 countries.